AUTHOR ID

Name: Kaye Umansky

Likes: Cheese, snow, happy music, cats, reading, writing, elephants.

Dislikes: Blancmange, drizzle, sad days, being stuck on a packed train, crocodiles.

3 words that best describe me:
Noisy. Big. Cheerful.

A secret not many people know:
I pretend I don't know how to work things (like the CD player) so someone else will do it for me while I sit on the sofa and eat nuts.

ILLUSTRATOR ID

Name: Mike Phillips

Likes: Cricket, books and my comfy chair.

Dislikes: Exercise, vegetables and sand in my shorts.

3 words that best describe me:
Short. Round. Fun.

A secret not many people know:
Don't tell anyone, but under my hat I'm bald!!

To Luke

Contents

Chapter 1

One Big Happy Family

Lardine

You know what makes me mad? I'll tell you. It's that everyone's on Cinderella's side. Just because she's pretty and ended up marrying Prince Florian, they all go "Ah! Bless!" and send her fan letters in the post. She gets other stuff as well. Posh dresses. Glass shoes. Flowers. Cake. Invitations to all the best balls.

My name's Lardine. I'm Cinderella's stepsister and my other sister's called Angula. I'm the soft, cuddly sister. Angula's all thin and sharp and bony. Just like a coat-stand.

No one ever sends me and Angula cake. What we get is lots of letters from people who don't like us – and they tell us so too. "Hate mail", the postman calls it. We don't get any invitations to balls. Not after what happened at the last one.

I said Cinderella's pretty. She is, in a boring sort of way. Long golden hair. Big blue eyes. Tiny, silly little feet. That sort of thing. Angula and I hated her from the first moment we saw her. We'd have hated her even more if we'd known she had a Fairy Godmother. But we didn't know that, not then. And back then, she was just plain Ella. It was me that gave her her new name – the one that's stuck – Cinderella.

"Come, darlings," said Mummy, on the day we moved into Stepdaddy Hardup's house. "Here we all are – a new happy family. I want you both to meet your new stepsister, Ella. I'm sure you'll all be good friends."

Angula and I looked at each other. We don't even like each other much, but we knew right now we needed to team up.

"Hello," said Cinderella with a shy smile. She put out her hand. We both looked at it as if she was passing us a dead fish. We did not shake hands with her and so she dropped it again.

Round One to us!

"Ella's bedroom is next to yours," said Mummy. "Won't that be nice?"

No. It wouldn't.

"I'm not sharing with Lardine," said Angula. "Her feet smell."

"So do yours," I snapped. Well, they do. Badly.

"Well, I don't snore," said Angula.

"Yes, you do," I said. She does. Very loudly.

"I'll scream if I don't get a room of my own," said Angula.

"And I'll sulk," I said. I would too. I really would.

"Don't worry," said Mummy. "We'll work something out."

Round Two!

At that moment, Stepdaddy Hardup came rushing into the room. He was grinning from ear to ear and rubbing his hands together. He still had a flower in his jacket from the wedding.

Angula and I were in our dresses from the wedding, our bridesmaid's frocks. My dress was too tight, and that put me in a bad mood. Angula's shoes were too small for her great big feet so she wasn't happy.

"Ah!" said Stepdaddy Hardup. "The girls have met at last. What d'you think, eh, Ella? It'll be fun having two new sisters, won't it, poppet?"

"Yes," said Cinderella. "I'm sure it will, Daddy."

She didn't sound as if it would. I don't think she liked the idea at all. Mummy said Cinderella didn't want her father to get married again. She didn't come to the wedding, anyway. She said she'd stay home and help get tea ready.

We think she was jealous because me and Angula were bridesmaids and she wasn't. Stepdaddy Hardup wanted her to be, but Mummy forgot to order her a dress.

"Good, good," Stepdaddy Hardup went babbling on, "Well, let's all go and have tea. Buttons has got a wedding feast ready for us in the front room."

Buttons is Stepdaddy Hardup's servant. I don't like him, and neither does Angula. He didn't help us off with our cloaks when we first came in. So we dropped them on the floor and shoved past him. We heard him tutting and muttering as he picked them up. Servants shouldn't tut. That's why I got a pair of scissors and snipped those stupid buttons off his jacket.

I have to admit the tea was nice. I ate seven sandwiches, three sausage rolls, five jam and cream scones, two helpings of trifle and a large hunk of wedding cake. Angula got stuck in as well. She may look like an ironing board but she can stuff a lot of food in her mouth. Even so, I think I'm just that bit better than her.

Cinderella hardly ate a thing. She just sat there, pushing a lettuce leaf around her plate. She didn't say a word.

"What's the matter, Ella? Aren't you hungry?" asked Mummy. She sounded cross.

"Not really," said Cinderella.

"You must eat, you know. Lardine and Angula have good manners. They always finish everything on their plates. Don't you, girls?"

"Yes, Mummy," we said both at the same time, our mouths full of cake.

"I do hope you're not letting her be a picky eater, Fergus," Mummy said to Stepdaddy Hardup. She gave one of her frowns. "Growing girls need plenty to eat. Have a sandwich, Ella."

"No, thank you," said our new stepsister. A tear trickled down her cheek and plopped onto the plate.

"She's crying," said Angula, with a sneer. She reached across Cinderella and grabbed the last doughnut. I'd had my eye on that. I wanted it. I poked her with a fork.

"Oh, dear," said Stepdaddy Hardup, looking upset. "Are you crying, Ella?"

"Just something in my eye, Daddy," said Cinderella. She patted her eyes with a napkin.

"I think you should leave the room," said Mummy. "We don't want a lot of fuss or drama at the table."

Cinderella stood up and ran out. Stepdaddy Hardup looked as if he was about to go after her, but then he saw Mummy look at him. He didn't move.

"Spoiled," said Mummy. "Spoiled rotten. She needs to be taken in hand."

"Just give her time," said Stepdaddy Hardup. "She'll get used to it, I'm sure."

"Oh, yes," said Mummy. "She'll get used to it all right. We'll make sure of that. Won't we, girls?"

"Oh, yes, Mummy," we sang. Well, we would.

Chapter 2
Teasing Cinderella
Angula

Well, Lardine's had her say in the last chapter, and now it's my turn. And just so you know, I did take that last doughnut, but Lardine took the last cream bun and finished up the trifle. And another thing – my feet may be big, but you should see her bottom.

On now to more important things.

We spent the next few weeks being mean to Cinderella. It was a lot of fun. We got her kicked out of her bedroom, of course. That was easy. Mummy told Stepdaddy Hardup that it was stupid, Cinderella having such a big room. Cinderella pretended she didn't mind. She said she'd sleep down in the kitchen, by the fire, with the cat. She said she liked looking into the glowing cinders in the fire. That's when we started to call her Cinderella – after the cinders. I came up with the name. Lardine says it was her, but that's a lie.

Cinderella started helping Buttons with all the jobs in the house. She seemed to like it, and even sang as she worked. We said "no way" to that. We told her she had a voice like a bull-frog. We said she wasn't to dance with the broom either, or make friends with little mice. Her soppy ways made us sick, we said. We took bets on who could make her cry first.

We cut holes in her dresses, and told Stepdaddy Hardup it was moths. We threw away her shoes. We gave all her combs and ribbons away to a jumble sale.

In the end, she didn't eat at the table with us because Mummy said she was too picky and it was getting on everyone's nerves. Stepdaddy Hardup got a bit upset about this, but he couldn't do anything because he's so poor. Mummy's the one with the money.

Mummy was happy we were so mean. She said Cinderella needed to get real. She said children with no brothers or sisters got their own way too much and it was bad for them. Cinderella had to learn. Stepdaddy Hardup tried to argue, but Mummy said she'd stop his pocket money if he didn't shut up.

Cinderella pretended she was happy, but we often caught her snivelling to Buttons. Buttons hated us even more since we cut his buttons off. We didn't care. We hated him too. We kept dropping things on purpose, so he'd have to pick them up. We ordered him to make us snacks in the middle of the night. We took the key to the kitchen cupboard and one day, when he was out, we muddled up all the jars. He keeps them all tidy. He couldn't say much, because he knew we could get him sacked.

We didn't want to get Buttons sacked. We were having so much fun being mean to him.

Mummy took Lardine and me shopping for new dresses. We didn't take Cinderella. I don't think she wanted to come anyway. Well, she'd have looked silly. She'd have had to walk into all the fancy shops in bare feet and rags. We left her cleaning the oven. We had a lovely day. We bought lots of gowns and jewels and ate cream cakes with cherries on the top.

On Cinderella's sixteenth birthday, we bought her an apron.

There was a bit of a fuss that day. Mummy saw Stepdaddy Hardup sneak along to the kitchen with a parcel.

"What's that you've got there, Fergus?" said Mummy when she saw him creep past the door.

"It's a present for Ella," said Stepdaddy Hardup. He went all pink and embarrassed.

"She's had her present," said Mummy.

"I know, dearest. But I thought her clothes were looking a little shabby. I got her a new gown."

"I see," said Mummy. "And whose money paid for it, may I ask?"

"Yours, dearest," said Stepdaddy Hardup, in a small voice.

"I thought so," Mummy went on. "And what have I said about spoiling children?"

"But I thought, as Lardine and Angula have just had new dresses ..." Stepdaddy tried to answer back.

"That's different," Mummy said firmly. "Lardine and Angula have to look good when they go visiting. But Cinderella spends all her time in the kitchen or roaming in the forest. She'll ruin a nice dress. Give it to me, I'll take it back and get a refund."

"But ..."

"Give it to me, Fergus."

So Stepdaddy handed it over. Lardine and I smirked at each other. Things were going really well.

Chapter 3
The Invitation
Lardine

That last chapter was rubbish. It wasn't Angula who came up with the name, it was me. And it was me who cut the buttons off as well. Angula does tell lies.

The invitations to the ball arrived on a Saturday morning. Angula and I were having a lie-in. Mummy had ordered Buttons to bring up our breakfasts on a tray. There are 95 steps between our rooms and the kitchen. You could hear Buttons puffing. It was great.

I stared at the tray. There was something else on it as well as my sausage, bacon, eggs, tomatoes, fried bread, mushrooms, beans, toast, jam, honey, pancakes, muffins, croissants, crumpets, and tea. There was a big envelope with a gold border all round it.

"What's that?" I asked.

"Arrived in the post," said Buttons without looking at me.

"Give!" I ordered. I snapped my fingers. He handed it over.

I opened it up. How happy I was when I saw what was inside.

"An invitation! I'm invited to the Prince's ball!" I shouted. "Hear that, Angula? I've got an invitation to the palace!"

"Me, too!" yelled Angula. She'd come into my room and was waving an envelope about also. I jumped out of bed, and the breakfast tray spilled all over the floor. We danced around the room.

When we heard that Cinderella was invited too we weren't happy about that. Nor was Mummy.

"She can't go, Fergus," she told Stepdaddy Hardup. He was standing in the hall with Cinderella's envelope in his hand.

"Why not?" he said. "Lardine and Angula are going, aren't they?"

"Of course. That's different. Prince Florian is looking for a wife. Ella can't marry him.

She doesn't know how to mix with posh people."

"But she's got an invitation," Stepdaddy said.

Mummy leaned across, took the envelope from his hand and ripped it in half.

"No, she hasn't," she said.

Angula and I smirked and headed for the kitchen.

Cinderella had her cloak on. About to go off on one of her boring walks, where she talks to little furry animals and helps poor old peasant women carry their bundles. We know, because we spy on her through a telescope sometimes.

"Guess what?" I said. "We're going to a ball at the palace and you're not. We're invited by Prince Florian."

"Well, I hope you enjoy yourselves," said Cinderella.

"Oh, we will," said Angula. "I intend to waltz with him all evening and make him fall in love with me while Lardine pigs out on cake."

"I don't think so," I said. "I think he'd sooner waltz with me than dance with someone who looks like a coat-stand and has feet like Cornish pasties."

"Oh, yes?" Angula screeched, "He'd need super long arms to get round your waist."

That made me rather annoyed. But I let it go. We needed to pick on Cinderella, not each other.

"Where are you going, Cinderella?" I asked.

"Not to play net-ball," sang Angula. "Or foot-ball. Or volley-ball. No balls where you're going, that's for sure."

Both of us cracked up at this.

"I'm going into the forest to gather kindling," said Cinderella.

"My, what an exciting life you lead," I said.

"Why don't you just leave her alone," muttered Buttons. He was sitting on a bench polishing shoes.

"Mind your own business, servant!" snapped Angula. She dipped her fingers in the boot polish and wiped them in his hair.

We're really, really good at this sort of thing.

Chapter 4
Getting Ready
Angula

Lardine's only half right. I'm the one who's good at saying nasty things. I'm the queen of the cutting remark. Lardine's just a beginner.

Anyway. We both had a wonderful time getting ready for the ball. We went shopping again, and Mummy bought us two wonderful ball gowns.

Well, mine was wonderful. It was purple (my favourite colour) with orange ribbons. Lardine's was a nasty yellow mustard colour with acid green ribbons. They didn't have a big enough size for her, so she was bursting out of it, as always.

We got new shoes too, and new fans and handbags and tiaras. Mummy said she didn't care how much she spent as long as the Prince fancied one of us. We had our hair done in a really expensive salon called "Hair We Are". I had mine swept up high on my head to show off my swan-like neck. Lardine went for blonde ringlets. The hairdresser left the dye on her hair too long, and it went a bit green. Lardine looked like a clump of seaweed had washed up on her head.

On the night of the ball, we made Cinderella come up and help us get ready. She pulled our laces tight (Lardine's had to be really tight). Then she put on our make-up for us and jammed our feet into our new high heeled shoes. My shoes pinched a bit because the shop didn't have size 11. But as Mummy said, you have to suffer a bit to be beautiful.

Mummy and Stepdaddy Hardup were waiting for us when we swept down the stairs. We looked fantastic!

"Darlings!" said Mummy. "How lovely you look! Don't they look fabulous, Fergus?" She gave him a hard poke in the ribs.

"Yes, indeed," said Stepdaddy Hardup. "Lovely." But he wasn't even looking at us. He was staring up at Cinderella, who was leaning over the banister. She was all sad and dreamy.

"Well, come along then," Mummy said. "The coach is waiting. We don't want to be late."

"Right," said Stepdaddy Hardup. "Yes, I suppose we must be off. Um – I'm sorry you're not coming, poppet."

"That's all right, Daddy," said Cinderella. "I'll have a nice evening in with Buttons, and an early night. I'll be fine."

And off we went. I was glad to leave that sad-o Cinderella behind.

We didn't know about the Fairy Godmother back then. If we'd known what was going to happen, we'd have locked Cinderella in the cellar and gagged her too, so she couldn't call out. But, sadly, we didn't.

All the way to the palace, Mummy kept going on and on about how we should be with royalty. She told Lardine not to eat too much. That's like telling a pig to go easy on the swill.

Then she said we had to agree with everything the prince said. She told us to curtsy low and laugh in tinkling, high voices. We had to flutter our fans and elbow other girls out of the way. There was going to be a lot of competition, Mummy said, so we had to make sure we got in first.

The palace is on top of a hill. It has high towers and a lake in the gardens, with orange fish in. It was all lit up, and the courtyard was crammed with coaches. Footmen were running around helping the guests out of the carriages.

Lardine slipped when she got out of our coach and fell in a heap. Her dress split down the side. I thought it was really funny and I laughed and laughed, but Mummy was a bit cross. She said it didn't look good.

Then Mummy wasn't too pleased when I slapped a footman across the ear with my fan. Well, he hadn't warned me to put my head down as I came out of the coach and I'd cracked it on the door.

It hurt. My head was sore and it was all the footman's fault. So why shouldn't he have a sore head too?

Mummy said the prince had soppy soft views about how to treat servants, and he might have seen me.

Anyway, I pushed my tiara over the bump on my head and Lardine held her bag over the rip in her dress. We were ready. Time for the ball!

Chapter 5

The Ball

Lardine

Just a few things before I start my chapter. Angula does not have a swan-like neck. She has a stork-like neck, which is something very different. And her dress was no way as nice as mine. But let's get on with the story.

Prince Florian was handsome, in a powdery sort of way. He was dressed from head to foot in powder blue. He had a white powder wig and a face with powder all over it. He stood next to the king and queen and greeted everyone on their way in. There was a long queue. I bull-dozed my way to the front. Angula came looming along behind me and tried to trip me up. A few people tut-tutted at us, but we didn't care.

"Miss Lardine Hardup!" a footman called out.

"Good evening, Miss Lardup," said Prince Florian.

"It's Hardup," I said. "Get it right."

Mummy began to cough. A lot. You're not meant to correct royalty.

"I beg your pardon, Miss Hardup," the prince said.

"Oh, do call me Lardine," I answered and I batted my eyelashes and made a curtsy. My dress ripped a bit more, but I don't think the prince noticed. Angula pushed me out of the way. She couldn't wait for her turn.

"Miss Angula Hardup," shouted the footman.

"Pleased to meet you," said Prince Florian.

"But not as pleased, happy and glad as I am to meet you, Prince Florian," said Angula. How smarmy was that! "I hope I can ask you for the first dance this evening?"

"Actually, I was about to say that," I chipped in, in a loud voice. I shoved Angula out of the way. The prince didn't get a chance to reply. Just then another footman told everyone that the food was ready. We all rushed towards where it was set out, and we nearly got trampled.

Well, I have to say that we did our fair share of trampling too. The food looked very delicious, and we wanted first grabs.

The orchestra started to play and the dancing began. People began to whirl around the dance floor. Prince Florian didn't, because he was still stuck in the welcome line. He had to greet all the stuck-up show-offs who thought they were in with a chance.

Mummy came up to me. She had left Stepdaddy Hardup over by a potted plant. He was nibbling on a cheese straw, looking sad.

"Now's your chance," she hissed behind her fan. "The prince is almost done. As soon as that last girl goes, don't mess about. Get in there!"

We were going to do just that. Both Angula and I were ready to rush up and grab the Prince's arms and drag him onto the dance floor. But we didn't. Something really odd happened next.

"Miss Terry Stranger," the footman called out.

Everyone looked round. The orchestra stopped playing. Standing there, in the doorway, was a dream of beauty. Well, if you like that sort of thing. I don't like all those dippy, girly colours.

The dream of beauty was dressed all in pale pink. Her gown had pearls sewn all over it. There were more pearls in her curly golden hair. She held a velvet mask over the top part of her face. When she moved forward, you could see that she wore teensy little glass slippers on her feet.

The crowd murmured. Who was this beautiful stranger with the strange-sounding name? And why the mask?

"Show-off," snarled Angula. For once, I couldn't agree more.

Prince Florian didn't think that. His mouth had dropped open and his eyes stuck out.

There's no point in telling you much about the rest of the evening. Prince Florian danced with the stranger all night. Whenever there was a gap between dances, all the rest of the girls crowded around. Maybe he'd turn to look at them? He didn't.

Angula and I didn't bother. We decided to just eat a lot and give Miss Stranger mean looks whenever she waltzed by. There was no point in rushing up to Prince Florian and grabbing him. It was as if he was under a spell.

But Mummy wouldn't give up. She thought that Miss Stranger might leave early. If she did, we'd still be in with a chance of the last waltz. As it turned out, Mummy was right.

When midnight came, there was a bit of a fuss. Miss Terry Stranger came to a stop, right in the middle of a polka. She gave a little cry, backed away from the prince, turned round, and ran off. She left one of her piddling little glass shoes lying on the floor behind her.

"Go, on," Mummy said and shoved, shoving us forward. "Grab him now! Go! Go!"

But Prince Florian wasn't in the mood for any more dancing. He fell to his knees, snatched up the shoe and held it to his chest. Then he burst into a long speech about coming around the next day and marrying the girl whose foot fitted the shoe. He added that it was a size three.

That's when Angula had one of her tantrums. When it comes to feet, she's very touchy. Trying to get her great big foot into that shoe would be like ramming a prize cucumber into a tiny baby food jar.

Angula gave a screech, hurled her fan onto the floor, jumped up and down on it and then kicked the food table. The table fell over with a huge crash, and all the food sprayed out all over everyone. Then she threw herself down onto the floor and began to scream and bite the carpet.

There's only one thing to do when Angula gets like that. I sloshed a jug of lemonade over her head. She jumped up and hit me with a spoon. She was still screaming. I wasn't having that.

I whacked her round the ear with my handbag. My bag was nice and heavy because

it was full of cake I'd put in it for later on.

Servants came running. There was a lot of fuss. The king and queen called Security.

Shortly after that we left. Mummy was angry because Prince Florian hadn't noticed us. Well, he had, but not in a good sort of way. Stepdaddy Hardup was fed up because he'd had a horrible evening. Angula was in a bad mood because her feet hurt and her hair was all sticky. I felt sick, because I'd stuffed myself too much.

Then I WAS sick.

It wasn't a good ride home.

Chapter 6

Back Home

Angula

For once, Lardine's chapter's right. When she threw up in my handbag, it was the last straw. In fact, I want to forget all about it and move on with the story.

When we got back, there was a large pumpkin by our front door. It was sitting at the bottom of the steps, which was odd. There were also some rats and some mice running around and making a lot of noise – squeaking and jumping. Did they know something we didn't?

A pumpkin? Cheeky mice? Rats with attitude? What was going on?

We found Cinderella in the kitchen. She was whispering something to Buttons. She looked flushed and was a bit out of breath. When she saw us, she and Buttons stopped whispering.

"Still up?" snapped Mummy. "I thought you were going to get an early night."

"I changed my mind," said Cinderella. "I had things to do." And she smiled an odd, secret smile.

She seemed cheerful. That was annoying. How dare she be happier than us?

"You're looking very pretty tonight, Ella," said Stepdaddy Hardup. That annoyed us even more.

"Thank you, Daddy," Cinderella said and smiled again. "Did you have a nice time at the ball?"

"All right, I suppose," said Stepdaddy Hardup. Then he saw Mummy look at him. "It was a very nice evening," he added quickly. "Most enjoyable. I think the girls had a good time, didn't you?"

"No," I snapped. "We didn't."

"What about Prince Florian?" asked Cinderella. "Do you think he enjoyed himself?"

"The less said about him the better," I growled. "He's got no taste, that one. No taste at all."

"Now then, Angula," said Mummy. "That's no way to talk about the man who might be your future husband."

"How do you make that out?" I snarled.

"Well, there's that shoe. Prince Florian's bringing it round tomorrow, remember? Both of you will get the chance to try it on. All is not lost."

"It's a size three," Lardine said. "I'm size 9, and Angula's size 11."

"So? Sit with your feet in a bucket of iced water," Mummy said. "Try and shrink them a bit. And in the morning, we'll rub in lots of butter, so they'll slip in easier."

"What do you mean – the shoe?" Cinderella asked, all innocent.

"Prince Florian spent all night dancing with a Miss Terry Stranger," Stepdaddy Hardup told her. "No one knew who she was. She ran off in a hurry and she left a glass shoe behind. Prince Florian says he'll marry the one whose foot fits it."

"Really?" said Cinderella. She looked at Buttons. Something was going on, but I didn't know what.

"What's this all over the floor?" asked Mummy. She was bending down and pointing at the kitchen floor. We all looked down. There was sparkly stuff everywhere.

"What can it be?" said Stepdaddy Hardup. He dabbed at it with his finger. "Snail trails, do you think?"

Of course, it was fairy dust, left behind by that stupid Godmother, but we didn't know that then.

"Well, I don't care what it is, some one needs to clean it up," said Mummy. And she stomped off upstairs to bed.

Lardine and I hung about a bit. We wanted to make Cinderella cry like we always do. But for once, it didn't work. She went on smiling in her odd, secret way, and Buttons was smirking and giggling too. There was something going on, but we didn't know what.

In the end, we went to bed.

Have you ever tried sleeping with your feet in a bucket of iced water? Don't.

Chapter 7
The Shoe
Lardine

The next morning, my feet were all blue and wrinkled. They looked like prunes. My toes were frozen together. I could hardly limp downstairs. Angula's were the same.

We sat in the kitchen, moaning like mad as Mummy rubbed best butter all over our toes.

"I can't feel a thing," I cried. Well, I couldn't.

"Even if I get the shoe on, I won't be able to walk in it," said Angula.

"You won't need to walk," Mummy told her. "Once Prince Florian asks you to marry him, they'll carry you around in a litter until your feet are better."

"Do we really need to do this?" asked Stepdaddy Hardup. "It's not the end of the world if they don't marry into royalty, is it?"

Mummy sent him out of the room. She doesn't like him poking his nose in at such an important time.

It was lucky we didn't have to wait long for Prince Florian. Our house isn't that far from the palace, so we were one of the first he visited.

There came a knock on the door, and Buttons went to open it. In came Prince Florian, still handsome. Today he was dressed in riding gear. He looked even better without his wig on. With him was a servant who was carrying the shoe on a red cushion.

"Right," said Prince Florian. "Let's get this over and done with. Which of you ladies is first?"

"Me!" we both yelled. "Me! Meeeee!"

"Now, now, girls," Mummy said as she hid the butter behind her back. "I'm sorry they're so rude, your Highness. It's just that they're both so keen."

"Tell you what, we'll toss a coin for it," said Prince Florian, and he took a penny out of his pocket. Angula chose heads and I chose tails. Heads won.

The servant took the shoe from the cushion and knelt by Angula's feet. Angula closed her eyes and crossed her fingers.

"Push, darling!" cried Mummy. "Never mind the pain! Push!"

As I thought, she couldn't even fit her toes in. The little glass shoe just dangled on the end of her big toe. It looked so stupid.

Angula gave a loud screech, kicked the glass shoe off and went off on one of her tantrums. She fell to the floor and kicked her feet around.

Then it was my turn. My feet aren't as big as Angula's, but I take a double E fitting. All the ice cubes and butter in the world weren't going to do the trick. I knew that just by looking. No way was my foot going to fit.

I went into a sulk. Angula does tantrums, I do sulking. We each have our own way of doing things.

"Well that was a waste of time," said Prince Florian. He was looking glad about that, which made me sulk even more. "Anyone else?"

"No!" we chanted.

"Yes," said a sweet little voice from the doorway. "Me. Can I try it on, please?"

"You?" I scoffed. "You weren't even there."

"Clear off, Cinderella, you're not wanted!" snapped Angula.

But the prince was staring at her in a funny way. His eyes were sticking out again. The servant ran up with the shoe.

It fitted. Wouldn't you know?

We all stood frozen. How could this be? Then Mummy passed out.

A fitting end to a horrible morning.

Fitting. Get it?

Chapter 8
The Happy Ending
Cinderella

You haven't heard from me so far. Well, that's how it should be. After all, this is my stepsisters' story. But I thought I should have a quick word, just to tell you what happened next. I don't think Lardine or Angula will.

What happened next was, Florian and I got married, and there was gladness and joy all across the land. He's a very nice man, and we're truly happy.

My Fairy Godmother came to the wedding, of course, and so did Buttons. They both enjoyed telling my stepmother and sisters what happened the night of the ball. They told them about the pumpkin coach and the mice and the magic fairytale dress and ... well, you know the story. Buttons said their faces were a picture when they worked out that Miss Terry Stranger was little old me.

Daddy got a divorce. He seems a lot happier. He lives with us in the palace now. He and Buttons have got into fishing, and spend a lot of time with the goldfish, down by the palace lake.

Florian was very upset when he heard how mean my stepfamily had been to me. He wouldn't let them stay in his kingdom. The last I heard, they were living in a rented bungalow next door to a fish finger factory somewhere very cold. Siberia, I think. I've written them some letters, but I never get a reply.

I suppose it serves them right – well, they were really horrid to me – but I'm not the sort to care. What's the point? I married the prince. I'm the one with the happy ending.

Post script

Lardine: Well, we told it in our own words.

Angula: We did.

Lardine: Do you think people will like us more now?

Angula: No. Do we care?

Lardine: No. Let's go and read our hate mail.

THE END

Barrington Stoke would like to thank all its readers for commenting on the manuscript before publication and in particular:

Lauren Bennet	Riccardo Kypernides
Josephine Cox	Jayesh Maru
Rowan Davis-Marks	Emily McGhee
Meghna Deshmukh	Hannah McLaughlin
Janet Dobney	Tariq Raheem
Wagner Gloria	Matt Robinson
Dev Halai	Callum Tibbitts
Hattie Jones	Conor Williets
Yvonne Keeping	Mrs Williets

Become a Consultant!

Would you like to give us feedback on our titles before they are published? Contact us at the email address below – we'd love to hear from you!

info@barringtonstoke.co.uk
www.barringtonstoke.co.uk